The Ch...
Cassidy's Creek

Story by Wendy Graham
Illustrations by Mini Goss

Rigby PM
part of the Rigby PM Collection

U.S. Edition © 2001
Harcourt Achieve Inc.
10801 N. MoPac Expressway
Building #3
Austin, TX 78759
www.harcourtachieve.com

Text © 2000 Wendy Graham
Illustrations © 2000 Thomson Learning Australia
Originally published in Australia by Thomson Learning Australia

10 9 8 7
09 08 07

The Creature of Cassidy's Creek
    ISBN 0 7635 7453 8

Printed in China by 1010 Printing International Ltd.

Contents

Chapter 1   The Groaning   4

Chapter 2   In the Dead of Night   9

Chapter 3   Strange Occurrences   12

Chapter 4   What's Lurking in the   17
              Cellar?

Chapter 5   Eyes in the Dark   21

Chapter 6   The Thing in the Cellar   26

Chapter 7   Trapped!   30

Chapter 1

The Groaning

Kevin stretched out on the bed. Here he was, staying at Grandma's old farmhouse at Cassidy's Creek for a whole week— where nothing ever happened.

He took his pencil and began to fill in a puzzle.

Suddenly he stopped writing. What was that? A peculiar, low groan had broken the silence ... There it was again!

He jumped up and ran out of the room, shouting, "Grandma!"

"What is it, Kevin?" asked Grandma, almost spilling her cup of tea.

"Grandma, I heard a really weird groaning sound. Did you hear it?"

"No," she said, smiling. "It's probably just a branch scraping on the window."

But Kevin had a strange feeling about the groaning noise. And he suspected it had come from the cellar.

His eyes moved toward the little door to the cellar. He knew that behind the door the rickety, wooden steps led down. The sliding bolt on the door was usually locked, but he noticed now that it had been pulled back.

Kevin opened the door and peered down the stairs. A strange smell came up from the depths. His hand groped at the cellar's light switch, but it didn't work.

Pushing the door shut, he quickly slid the bolt across. There was something there … he was certain.

Behind that door.

Down the steps.

In the dark.

Chapter 2

In the Dead of Night

Kevin woke suddenly.

Music! He could hear the piano! Here in the house in the middle of the night, someone was playing the piano!

His heart thumped against his chest.

The jangle of notes abruptly stopped.

Kevin sprang out of bed. At his door he paused, listening. A gentle snore came from Grandma's room.

In his bare feet, he tiptoed toward the living room.

He stared at the piano ... Nothing.

Then he glanced at the cellar door. He knew he'd slid the bolt across yesterday, but now the little door was ajar!

Kevin turned and ran back to bed.

Chapter 3

Strange Occurrences

The next morning, Kevin wondered about his fears of the night before.

"Grandma," he said, at breakfast, "I had the strangest dream. I dreamed somebody was playing the piano in the middle of the night."

Grandma placed two steaming plates of freshly cooked pancakes on the table. "That old piano needs a jolly good tuning," she remarked and poured syrup over her pancakes.

Kevin fell silent. Then his eyes widened as he noticed something.

It was only an apple. But it was on the floor, and it had a few bites out of it.

It wasn't there last night!

There must be a simple explanation, thought Kevin. He decided not to mention it to Grandma. No use alarming her.

After breakfast, he checked the kitchen window. It was tightly locked. Then he checked the living room window. It too was locked.

That's when he noticed that the vase of flowers on the end table had been tipped over.

Kevin's skin began to tingle. He glanced over at Grandma, who was busy clearing the breakfast table.

He hurriedly mopped up the puddle of water with his table napkin, and pushed the flowers back into the vase.

Could Grandma have knocked a vase over without noticing? he wondered. And maybe she had taken the apple and forgotten about it, then it rolled off the table.

But what about the groaning noise he'd heard yesterday? And the midnight piano player?

Then he saw something else. The curtains—they weren't like that yesterday! One side was hanging off the curtain rail.

His heart missed a beat. Okay, okay, Kevin said to himself. The place was securely locked. There was nowhere to hide, he was certain.

Except for the cellar.

Chapter 4

What's Lurking in the Cellar?

Grandma went outside to plant some herbs in her vegetable garden. As soon as she'd gone, Kevin hurried to the cellar door. Wait a minute! It was shut again, but the sliding bolt was open. He clearly remembered seeing the door ajar last night.

He raced outside. "Grandma," he asked, out of breath, "did you go into the cellar?"

"I started to, dear. I was taking down some old books," she said, "but the light didn't work. Now, Kevin, don't you even think about going down there. There's only old junk, and lots of spiders. Why don't you climb that old apple tree? You can see Cassidy's Valley from the top."

Kevin needed time to think, so he swung his leg up and began to climb. Just as he'd nestled into a comfortable fork in the branches, something nearly made him fall out of the tree. Out of the corner of his eye he saw movement in the front window of the house.

Kevin stared hard, but all was still. Only the impression of it stayed with him. It was faint but definite, like the brush of a cat's tail. Or a wisp of smoke that vanishes before your eyes.

He swung down from the tree and marched toward the house.

Chapter 5

Eyes in the Dark

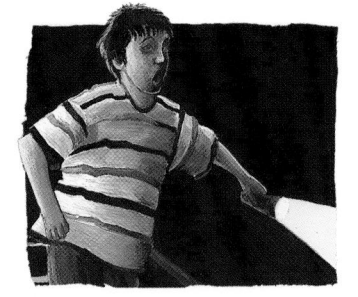

Kevin grabbed the flashlight from the kitchen drawer, went straight to the cellar door, and swung it open.

"HEY!" he yelled down the stairs in his bravest voice.

"HEY! HEY! HEY! HEY!" his voice echoed back.

Moving down a couple of steps, he flicked the beam of light around the dark cellar.

Dusty bottles of wine lined one wall. A broken bike, a lumpy mattress, and piles of books covered the floor.

Kevin wrinkled his nose. There was that strange smell again.

Then he gasped. Two eyes were staring at him from the darkness.

Kevin quickly backed out of the cellar door, shut it, and slid the bolt across. He burst out the front door and sprinted across the lawn.

"Grandma, there's someone or something in the cellar. I saw it!" he yelled. "There were eyes looking straight at me!"

"Oh, Kevin," Grandma said. "That sounds like another dream of yours!"

"No, Grandma, it's true," said Kevin. "I heard that groaning and then the piano last night and there was an apple on the floor and a vase was knocked over and the curtains were nearly pulled down—" He stopped for a breath, then hurried on, "and when I was in the tree, I saw something move in the house. There's something in there, Grandma, I saw it!"

"What an imagination!" Grandma smiled, and, shaking her head, she picked up the garden fork and began to prod at the soil.

Kevin knew there was only one thing to do. He went to the shed and took out an old tarp.

Back in the house, staring at the cellar door, he took a deep breath. Then he slid the bolt across, pulled the door open, and clicked on the flashlight. Crouching and holding the tarp, he stepped down ...

Into the dark cellar.

Chapter 6

The Thing in the Cellar

Down the steps Kevin went, one by one, shining the flashlight ahead of him. He felt sure he was being watched.

Suddenly, right in front of him, there was a flurry of movement.

He yelled and lunged forward. He quickly threw the tarp over the thing, then flung himself on top of it. It was trapped! He could feel the creature struggling, and hear its muffled, furious noises.

That's it! Kevin realized. The groan he'd heard yesterday!

Fear made him strong. He held onto the struggling creature with all his might.

A beam of light beamed from the cellar door at the top of the steps. He decided to make a rush for the door and lock the thing in the cellar again. He'd convince Grandma to help.

But first he had to let go!

Carefully, his fingers crept to the edge of the tarp. Then, suddenly, he flung it back like a bullfighter's cape and leaped for the stairs at the same time. The thing didn't chase him.

Halfway up the stairs, Kevin looked over his shoulder.

Terrified eyes stared back at him. A big, gray opossum with matted fur and pointy ears sat, trembling.

Kevin breathed a sigh of relief.

Chapter 7

Trapped!

"He's a big fellow, all right," Grandma said. "I wonder how he got inside." They stood looking at the opossum caught in the old rabbit cage. It had been easy to trick him in there with some cut-up fruit.

Kevin helped Grandma lift the cage into the back of her old pickup truck, and soon they were bumping down the dusty drive on their way to release the opossum in the forest.

Kevin sighed. What a relief! Now there'd be no more strange happenings. He was rather pleased with himself. He should be a detective!

And yet ... something was still bugging him. Something wasn't quite right.

Kevin thought about all that had happened and his scalp began to prickle ...

When he was in the apple tree, he'd seen movement in the house. That's when he'd come inside and found out what it was.

But how could the opossum have been moving around the house? Because right then it had been locked in the cellar!